THE

DUNGEONS

OF

SUFFERING

The Adventures of Johnny McGinnis

Book 2

Written By:

Mickey Wilcox

August, 2013

www.mickeywilcox.org

www.mickeywilcox.org

2

"I will praise you O Lord, with all my heart.

I will tell of all your wonders.

I will be glad and rejoice in you;

I will sing praise to your name, O most high.

My enemies turn back;

They stumble and perish before you.

For you have upheld my right and my cause;

You have sat on your throne, judging righteously.

You have rebuked the nations and destroyed the wicked;

You have blotted out their names forever and ever."

www.mickeywilcox.org

3

CONTENTS

www.mickeywilcox.org

CHAPTER 1

PAUL AND SILAS EXPERIENCE

I came to lying on the floor. My hands tied behind my back and my feet tied together. There was a rag tied around my mouth to gag me. My head felt as though it were ready to explode. I was having trouble focusing my eyes. With a great deal of effort I could make out Tom lying next to me. I couldn't see where Patty was. I heard men talking in a strange language. I had heard it before but right now I couldn't place it. I moved my head to try and look around. It hurt so bad I thought it might explode at any time. I finally got a look at the three men standing at the wheel. Pirates! We had been taken by pirates. They looked small and slight yet well-muscled. The best I could do was place them from somewhere around south-east Asia. This wasn't looking good at all. Them keeping us alive meant that it was going to be really bad for us. Normally they just kill the owners when they take a boat. If they were keeping us alive it was because they were going to make money off of us, either in the slave trade or more likely, by cutting out our organs and selling them. Kidneys brought good money on the open market. So did livers and practically everything inside of us. We would be parted out like a used car.

I began to pray. I prayed for courage and strength. I prayed that God would display His might. I also prayed that if God wanted to call me home now, that would be good with me, just don't let them cut me apart piece by piece to sell on the market. I asked Him to make it a heroic death, so as to glorify his name.

I opened my eyes just in time to see them drag Tom down below. Then one of the men grabbed my legs and started dragging me down below also. They pushed me into the forward cabin where I had been sleeping and closed the door. It was dark and I could feel Tom and someone else that I suspected was Patty. Only God can deliver us. His word says so, and it is His word that I live and die by now. I am a Kingdom man. I serve the Lord Jesus Christ. With that, I began to praise him out loud. It was muffled because of the gag, but I praised Him as loudly as I could. It wasn't long before Tom began to join me in a muffled praise session.

After a few moments, I asked Tom how Patty was. I was anxious about asking that question. I remembered the gunfire I had heard earlier and her scream. Tom relaxed me when he said that she was alright as far as he could tell. She was unconscious but he could feel her rhythmic heartbeat. Then he began to praise God again. I joined in with him. The more we praised God the louder we got. It wasn't long before a big brute of a man came barging into the cabin where we were held as prisoners and made it clear that we were to be quiet. In the light that poured into the cabin, I took stock of the situation.

We were in a "v" berth cabin with closets at the head of each bed and the door in the middle of the two closets. Tom and Patty were on the port side of the cabin; which means the left hand side when you are looking ahead from the cockpit. Patty lay more or less on her face alongside the bed. Tom was at her feet on his knees. I was opposite Tom with my hands tied tightly behind my back and sitting cross-legged or Indian style as I knew it by. My safari vest was above Tom's head on the bed. I could tell my stuff had been gone through. That was the last thing I saw before the guard punched me in the side of the face. I went down and hit the floor hard. I lay there for a moment with my eyes closed.

In the movies, the hero in this situation would look up and spit in the guards face. I wasn't sure if I was going to be able to move my face! That man hit hard! Slowly I lifted my body back up to see the man standing over me. I suddenly began to laugh. Not really loud or obnoxious, just more of a smile and a chuckle. I couldn't help it. I started to say "Praise God," but I was rudely cut off by another punch to the side of the head. It would have helped if I could have turned to the other side. If he keeps punching me in the same spot he is going to break something.

How was I to tell him that I wasn't laughing at him? I was thinking of the teachings of our King as recorded in the book of Matthew where He said, "Blessed are you when people insult you, persecute you and falsely say all kinds of evil against you because of me. Rejoice and be glad, because great is your reward in heaven, for in the same way they persecuted the prophets who were before you."

I was just thinking that I hoped this counted because I sure didn't want a good beating to go to waste! That's when I began to laugh.

As I was face down on the floor for a second time, I heard Tom say something in a different language. It must have angered the guard because I looked up just in time to see Tom get punched. The guard said something then closed the door.

Once again, it was dark. Through a numbed and swollen face, I asked Tom if he was okay. He said he was fine, although it took him a moment to respond and he sounded a little bit woozy when he did.

"I told him that he didn't need to be so cruel, that we were going to be cooperative." Tom said painfully. "That's when he punched me and told me that we needed to shut up."

"Any ideas?" I asked.

"Praise God and wait for his deliverance," replied Tom.

With that, we went back to singing praises. Our praises to God were not just songs, which was a good thing because I did not know the words to any songs completely. Our praises would often be declarations of God's greatness and power. We would make up our own songs and speak all the good things of who God is. Sometimes Tom would even quote Bible scripture. It was in this way that we found ourselves forgetting that we were prisoners and finding ourselves having a worship service. For the most part we were relatively quiet and reserved in our expressions of love towards God.

After a couple hours, maybe two or three, it was hard to estimate in the blackness of our cell; Patty began to stir. Quickly, Tom responded to her as best that he could, considering he was in the dark and tied up. Patty assured us and our repeated inquires that she was okay. She said that her hands were tied also and that her head hurt some, other than that she was pretty sure she was okay. She asked what had happened and Tom began to share with her all that she had missed.

I was amazed that she remained so calm. All the sweetness of spirit that she had before this incident seemed to still be there. Her first concern after that of Tom and I, was a concern for our captors. She asked in the most compassionate tone I have ever heard if any of them had been hurt. I was speechless at her question. What a great and godly woman Tom had married. Where I wrestled with thoughts of harm towards my captors, she demonstrated compassion towards them. How true it was that a godly woman was a jewel in a man's crown. Tom had to be tremendously proud of his wife.

I sat quietly in the darkness trying to allow Tom and Patty as much privacy as possible considering the circumstances. I spent my time praying silently. I started with a heart that desired God to free us, but it didn't take long before I really began to feel strongly that God didn't want us freed just yet, He wanted to do something great through this. So, I began to pray for courage and strength. I began to remember all the men and women of the Bible who faced such difficulties as we face now and I thought of their different qualities that were good and right. I began to pray for these same qualities in my life. As I did this, the words of one of my teachers in The Kingdom Disciple program, that I had recently graduated from, came to me: "Every situation we find ourselves in, is an opportunity for God to do something great. Our job is to seek out the guidance of the Holy Spirit and follow that guidance. When we do this, we are true kingdom men and women."

I had made a decision to follow Jesus anywhere and everywhere. Today, I get to follow through on that decision. I began to seek out the will of God in this situation. All He said to my spirit was to be patient and praise Him. So this is what I did. Quietly, so as not to disturb Tom and Patty, I began to praise God again. This time, with purpose; I was going to be used by God in a great way - it was time for a celebration! Before I realized it Tom and Patty joined in and began to praise God louder and louder. After a short while, the guard came in and started yelling something. Then he lashed out and punched me again, knocking me over. As if that were not enough, he began kicking at all three of us. Tom would throw his body in front of Patty trying to deflect and catch as many of the blows as possible. He succeeded for the most part, but a few blows did land on her. She lay on the floor weeping softly when the guard closed the door and retreated into the boat.

I sat there in silence as I listened to Tom reassure his wife that he loved her and that Jesus was still King. That's when I realized that at some point her weeping turned into a song of worship and praise of Jesus! She was quickly joined by Tom. I followed shortly afterward as I reflected how much God must love me to allow me to be in this situation with two strong and committed believers.

Within no time at all, our praise songs became loud and joyful again. Again, the guard opened the door and released his rage on us. Again we picked ourselves up and started all over. It wasn't a rebellious spirit. It became something that seemed to be beyond our control. No matter how many times the guard came in; no matter how much he beat us; no matter how many times we were knocked down; a joyful song rose up in us. When I would be beaten until dazed, I would slowly regain my senses and find myself already praising Jesus with my mouth!

After hours of praising Jesus and beatings by the guard, we all three eventually fell asleep due to exhaustion. Our bodies couldn't take anymore.

I awoke sometime later. My body was stiff and sore. I lay in the darkness thinking of Paul and Silas in prison for preaching the gospel. They stood in the innermost part of the prison which was probably more like a dungeon. By comparison, we probably had it a bit more comfortable. Here at least I had the carpet that padded the floor. There, they had a stone floor that was cold and hard. I had the warmth of the south Pacific; they had the cold and damp. Yet in the midst of all that, they still praised Jesus. In fact, God caused a great earth quake and the doors of the jail fell open. The guard who would have been publicly humiliated and executed for his prisoners escaping was about to commit suicide. He felt it was better to kill himself rather than to face what would surely come. That's when Paul yelled out to the guard that he and Silas were still there. Because of their willingness to stay in the prison instead of leaving the moment opportunity presented itself, they got to lead the guard's entire family to Jesus and witness the birthing of a new church.

It was after reflecting on this testimony of Paul and Silas, that I made the commitment to follow this through, no matter what, until these men either set me free or surrendered themselves to Jesus the King. Today they served the Dark Prince; soon they would serve the King of Glory! Again, the words of my instructor for the Kingdom Disciples program came to me: "A true kingdom man or woman of God always evaluates their situation based on kingdom goal and objectives. Never on their personal wants and desires. We follow the way of love. We are willing to joyfully endure all things for the sake of Christ and His kingdom."

I soon fell back asleep with great thoughts filled with joy and happiness. I would be as committed as Paul and Silas were. This was going to be alright! I was going to get through this; God was going to be glorified and His kingdom was going to grow! What a great God I serve.

I was awakened up with a kick to my shins. I was startled for a moment because I couldn't move my arms. "O yeah," I thought, "I'm still a prisoner." I realized that they had opened the ceiling hatch cover and the room was flooded with light. What a pleasant blessing that was.

The guard set down a large bowl that Patty used for mixing flour and ingredients for bread. It was filled with water. It sat in the middle of the floor between the three of us. Then the guard turned and closed the door as he left.

"Water," I said loudly, "Praise God!"

Tom leaned forward to get a drink when his wife scolded him. "Thomas Elwood!" She said, "I cannot believe you are going to drink without thanking God for such a wonderful blessing."

Isn't it strange how a wife can suddenly sound like a mother? Tom stopped dead in his tracks and looked up at his wife sheepishly. "You are right, dear. Forgive me."

Tom bowed his head as we all did, and he prayed, thanking God for this blessing of water and praising Him for caring for us. It reminded me that even something small like a drink was important to remember and honor God. This by itself was a witness to our commitment to Jesus.

CHAPTER 2

ANIMALS IN A CAGE

Later that afternoon, Tom said we were coming into a port or harbor. "By the sound of it," he said, "It's not that big. It's probably a private harbor. They will probably take us off here and put us in a jail or prison. The *Pearl of Love* will be taken away and sold. We may not see each other again. We should pray together while we still can."

We huddled together to pray and at least touch one another before we were taken off the boat. We each took a turn praying to God for each other and the men that took us captive. When it was my turn, I also prayed for Tom and Patty, and myself. I prayed for the men who took us and their families and the people of this place we were at. As I prayed, I began to recount my commitment to allow God to use me here and follow through with this. I prayed He would not abandon these people until they either let me go or they committed their lives to Christ.

When I finished, Tom said that it sounded like someone got a word from God. I explained to both of them what had happened last night. We all three began praising God for who He is.

We felt the boat stop against the pier or dock or whatever we had been brought alongside. We could hear the hustle and bustle of things going on outside. In just a moment, the door was opened and our guard waved us to get up. None of us could get up. We tried but our beaten and exhausted bodies would not cooperate with our will.   The guard roughly grabbed ahold of each of us in turn and forced us to our feet. As we climbed the couple of steps leading to the pilot house of the *Pearl of Love,* a rope collar with leash was dropped around our neck. A different man led each of us from the boat and onto the dock.

I looked around and saw less than one hundred people. They were all well-tanned, well-muscled, and well-armed. Even the few women I saw looked hardened. There were a couple women that looked under-nourished and poorly kept. They were probably slaves. There were several crude buildings built in the fashion of an island village. They were poorly constructed, but not by the standards of the hundreds of islands that dotted this region of the world.

We were led to the shore by our leashes. We offered no resistance. They took us under the nearest pavilion type structure where several men sat around a wooden table. We stood there for several minutes. Finally, a small framed man came quietly running up to one of the men at the table. He handed him a piece of paper. It was something from the boat, probably the insurance certificate.

The man at the table who received the paper said in a slow, calm and cruel voice; "Thomas?"

Tom just shook his head yes. Then the man said something in his language. Tom responded. Then they had a conversation that appeared to be getting more heated as they talked. Tom seemed to remain calm, but the other man at the table got louder and more animated as they went back and forth. The other men at the table started getting involved and they all kept yelling at Tom. Tom never changed his tone. He said less and less words until he was finally reduced to one word of which I am pretty sure was "No!"

One of the men even got up and began pushing Tom as he yelled in Tom's face. Tom calmly said the same word and the man punched him again. Tom's knees buckled and he dropped straight down. As his knees hit the ground, the man holding his leash jerked him back up. Tom took a slow breath and said a short sentence which made the man who just hit him even more furious. Just as he was about to punch Tom again, the man who received the papers said something that made him stop. He took his seat. The man who had the papers stood up slowly. He went to Patty and stroked her hair. He took one well-muscled arm and forced her to her knees. She offered no resistance as he did this. The man laid his hand over top of Patty's head and said something. I knew it was evil whatever it was. You could feel the evil here. This was a strong outpost of the Dark Prince.

Suddenly Patty said very clearly to Tom; "It doesn't matter what they do to me, you stand with Jesus and never back down!" Immediately the man punched her. She crumpled to the ground.

The man poured a warm beer over Patty's face until she regained consciousness. Then he reached down and took her by her hair. He pulled her back up to her knees and then he pulled out his pistol. It was an old .45 caliber ACP. I recognized it as an old Marine Corps issue pistol.   Same style; probably left here from World War 2. He put the pistol to the top of Patty's head as she knelt there. All at the same time, I heard Patty begin to sing a worship song, the man with the pistol say something to Tom, and Tom's eyes flooded with tears. Tom responded with a single word, and the gunman pulled the trigger.

Patty died instantly. Just before my knees gave out from under me at the terrible sight, I saw Tom collapse to the ground. As soon as I dropped to my knees gasping in horror at what had just happened, the man holding my leash began to jerk upwards on it. The man who had just shot Patty barked out some commands and the man jerking on my leash ran quickly to Patty's body. Suddenly everyone's attention was away from me. The spectators and all the armed men were completely ignoring me. There was an idling motor-boat parked at the dock unattended. The man who had just started it came running the moment the gunshot was heard. There was no one to guard me. Now was my chance. I turned to run. Immediately, my promise to God resounded in my head. I wasn't going to leave here until they either let me go or they gave their lives to Christ. I turned back around, tears streaming down my face, praying to God to help me. I was terrified. This wasn't at all how I had pictured any of this in my mind. I didn't think too hard about it then, but none of us were supposed to die. "O Lord," I cried, "help us!"

What could I do? I was a kingdom man; sold out in love with Jesus. To escape would be to back out on a promise I made to God. It would be to worry about my own skin and not the Kingdom of Jesus. Jesus called us to die to our self, our own desires. His purpose had to be more important than mine. I couldn't run, no matter how painful it was to stay. Anyway, if I ran, I would be turning my back on Tom. Poor Tom, he just lost his wife. How would he make it?

The man that held my leash and the man that held Patty's scooped up her body and carried it off. Two other armed men escorted Tom and I away. Tom walked as a dead man might walk. His face was expressionless as if no-one was home, but the lights were still on.

We walked through a winding street that was more like a path than a street. People gawked at us as we passed by, but nobody made a move to say or do anything to us. As we came around a set of buildings, we came to an area filled with cages. There were about a dozen. Most were filled with people. Here they separated Tom and I. They took Tom to the left. They took me to a cage directly in front of us. That's when the armed guard pushed me with his rifle into the cage. He padlocked it and then motioned for my hands. He untied me and slipped the collar off of my neck. It was my first time being able to move my hands since the pirates first took the *Pearl of Love*. My hands were red and swollen, almost purple. They were stiff and the returning blood to them made them hurt really badly. I sat down on the makeshift bamboo cot. I had never faced despair like this before. This situation looked hopeless. I hung my head into my red, pain swelled hands and wept.

I have no idea how many hours, days, or weeks passed. Once or twice a day they would bring a bowl of warm water and a large leaf filled with rice. The first couple times I ate what I could. After that I barely ate and I only remember drinking a few times when thirst overwhelmed me. I didn't get out of my cot except to use my toilet bucket that was already overflowing and fly covered when they put me in here. I wanted to be Patty; I wanted to be dead and not have to go through this anymore. It was more than I could bear. I had spent the first couple of days crying out to God for deliverance. I would try to remember all the scripture I had learned that were God's promises of deliverance. I tried praying for the other captives and even the harsh guards. Nothing happened; my life and situation seemed hopeless.

It was several days or so, I guess, when a guard came to get me. He yelled for me to get up, but I didn't move. I didn't want to move, I wanted to be dead and with Jesus and not suffer this anymore. This was more than a man could bare and it wasn't fair. The guard came into my cell and kicked me, yet I still didn't move. Then he pulled me out of my makeshift bamboo bed and across my floor, and out my door. He let go of me, letting me fall to the ground. Then he kicked me and I slowly got up. He put my collar and leash back on and guided me out of the prison cage areas. We got to an area near the jungle that was being cleared. I saw other ragged gloom-faced men and women cutting away at the jungle with machetes. My guard took off my leash and collar and handed me a machete and signaled for me to go and join the work crew. Slowly I walked forward. I had little strength and no motivation other than the men holding AK-47 machine guns. I looked around to see if I could see Tom as I worked, but I couldn't see him anywhere. "Maybe they killed him," I thought. "at least he would be with Patty in the presence of Jesus and not here in this cruel misery."

I had not been working long when I heard someone singing. I couldn't really recognize the voice, although it sounded a bit like Tom. Whoever it was sure was having a good day. He sounded really happy to be here. I turned to get a look at the oncoming voice. That's when my jaw went slack and I couldn't lift my arms. It was Tom. His face was badly beaten and bruised. He limped a little dragging his left leg as if it was hurt, but it was Tom. His face beamed with joy. He wasn't being pulled by his leash; he was walking as if he wanted to go to beat down the jungle for these vicious captors. As he came past me he said as if it were a part of his song; "Johnny, my son, have you forgotten who you are? Today is the day the Lord has made and I shall be glad and rejoice in it!"

I stood there slack-jawed and staring until one of the guards yelled at me getting my attention. Tom was crazy; he must have gone around the bend, as they say. But he wasn't and I knew it. I was the crazy one here. What Tom said was right; I had forgotten who I was. I turned back to the jungle lifting my weakened arms to swing the machete. I could still hear him singing through his swollen face and mouth. It was a little fainter now because they had put him on the opposite side of me and was some hundred feet away. I chuckled, than I thanked Jesus for the reminder and the encouragement. I asked Jesus for forgiveness as I worked slowly with the small amount of energy I had. My mind raced as if it had just been awakened from some long slumber. I had forgotten who I was. I am a kingdom man! Redeemed by the most high God, never to be forsaken by Him. Jesus is my king and He is fully aware of everything that goes on in my life. I had been allowing the Dark Prince to take my mind captive with all these gloomy, hopeless, despairing thoughts! I had allowed myself to believe that Jesus had forgotten me in this place. That was not the truth! Jesus promised to never forget me. He said He would never abandon me nor forsake me. I was his, a child of the King! I didn't have much strength from not eating for so long, but I began to sing and work with all the strength I had. This is the day the Lord has made and I will rejoice and be glad in it!

After a couple of hours of hacking away at the jungle with the dull machetes, the guards began to take us one by one back to our cages. We were soaking wet from the intense humidity. I only some shorts on.

No shirt or shoes. I was still wearing what I was wearing when they came aboard the *Pearl of Love* and took us captive.

As we were walking back to my jail cell, it began to rain. Almost in a moment, it went from a lightly overcast sky to a grey downpour. The rain came down in torrents. This time instead of being dragged, I was walking of my own accord. I had a smile on my face even though I had a rope collar around my neck and a rope leash to keep me. I praised God for the rain. It was refreshing to me and was washing all the sweat and grime off of me. What a blessing! I remembered Patty scolding Tom when we were about to drink the bowl of water we had been given. I began to laugh out loud. I praised Jesus even more. God is great!

The guard held my leash and carried a gun. He thought he was the one in charge and that he was making me move. This morning he was. Now it was different. He didn't realize it, but he was no longer the master and he wasn't leading, he was following and I was going to lead him straight to Jesus! I was so encouraged right then. It was all I could do to not stop and burst out laughing. When we got to my cell, I politely stepped aside so that my guard could open the door. When he did, I thanked him and bowed slightly. Then I smiled and stepped in. He looked at me questioningly as he removed my collar. He never took his eyes off of me as he backed away with one hand on his machine gun. You could tell that I was making him nervous. I couldn't hold back anymore. As he closed the door, I burst out laughing. I couldn't stop. He yelled something and came towards the cell, but I still couldn't stop laughing. The more upset he got the more I could only laugh. He spit at the ground in front of me and left quickly. I know he thought I was mad as a hatter, but I wasn't. I was so filled with the joy of Jesus, I was bubbling over. I shouted after him, "Jesus loves you and you're about to find that out!" Then I went back to my uncontrollable laughter.

Later, when they brought me my bowl of water and my leaf of cold sticky rice, I received it as if it were the best meal I had ever had. When the girl slid it in under my bamboo bars, I thanked her. I bowed my head and prayed over my meal, thanking Jesus for his provision for my nourishment. I took every bite slowly and sipped my water. Others around me drank their water as fast as they could and ate the rice as if it were the only food left on the planet. Some yelled profanities and threw the rice at our captors. I just observed all the goings on around me. I had missed so much in my mental captivity. It was so nice to be back in my right self, my redeemed self. Jesus was wonderful.

For the next several weeks our days stayed the same. We received a small portion of warm rice and warm water in the morning. Later we were taken from our cages and taken out to the jungle edge where we labored at cutting the jungle away. After several hours of labor, we were returned to our cages and feed a small portion of cold rice and warm water. As this time progressed I began to pick up more and more of their language. I learned enough that I was able to understand quite a bit of what was being said.

After some time, I was moved to a new set of cells. These were more of a block with eight cells connected together. There were two rows of four cells each. Each cell contained a large makeshift bamboo cot about six inches off the floor. Our bamboo floors were about two feet off of the dirt ground. Each cell had two men in it. I was moved in with a man named Robert. Robert was a retired investor. He was captured along with his 57 foot yacht named *Thor*. He had a wife, daughter, and a son-in-law. His wife used to cook for these bandits, as he called them, but he has not seen her in a long time. His daughter was sold to be a sex slave. She was young, only twenty-two and a newlywed. Jonathan, his son-in-law, tried to escape one day while they were building a building here and was captured. He was beaten ruthlessly. Later, he died from the beating. Robert said that when they first took him and his family, he agreed to file against the insurance that the boat had been sunk in a storm in the Pacific. *Thor* was insured for a million and a half. He figured that these bandits would take the money and release his family. They took the money all right, but they kept his family also.

Most of the stories from the others were the same. Boat captured, insurance demanded. Family kept, women sold or enslaved. Men kept for labor.

Tom was moved into the same cell complex as me. Our cells were catty-corner from one another. As soon as the guards left, after bringing Tom to our complex, we hurriedly embraced one-another through the bars. There were tears of joy as we praised God for each other. Tom pulled back after a long moment. He had a great big smile and he said "It's so good to see the man of God that came onto the *Pearl of Love* returned to me!"

'Forgive me," I said a little downcast as I remembered the depression I had fallen into.

"There is nothing for me to forgive brother," said Tom, "the Dark Prince was trying to take you captive and I just reminded you who you are. Let us rejoice in our Lord together!" With that we began to sing a praise song.

We sat in the corners of our cells with our backs to one another praising Jesus. At times one of us would stop singing and begin to pray, at other times we would both pray. It was good to worship together.

CHAPTER 3

PLANTING THE CHURCH

Every day from that point forward, Tom and I would come together in our corners to talk, pray, and worship. We would wait for each other to receive our meals then we would thank God for our meal and eat together. In the beginning, several of the men would ridicule us and make sarcastic remarks putting down Jesus. Some would yell out blasphemous things at times. Tom and I tried to take each incident in stride and smile pleasantly. It was important for us to remember that each one of these men had seen great hardship and terrible atrocities in their life here. They didn't understand the love of God or who this Jesus is that Tom and I serve. Occasionally, one of the men would ask why we could remain joyful in all of this or why we would thank Jesus for the brutal work we were given to do, or some such question like that. We used these as opportunities to share the truth of God's hope and love with all the men. It never seemed to go beyond that and always there was at least one man that would yell profanities and curse God.

Once when one of these teaching moments was going on, one of the men became completely out of control in his belligerence. He started throwing anything he could at us and was cursing God using every vial profanity he could think of. I just sat there quietly and prayed silently for the man. That's when we heard a voice. It was beautiful and calming and it made everyone go silent, including the man throwing the fit.

"Daddy!" said the voice of a young girl who was bringing our water. "Why are you cursing God? You taught me that Jesus loves us all the time. No matter what life looks like around us. You should be ashamed of yourself. Now stop that right now and act like the father I know."

All of us were quiet. All eyes were on the girl, and every ear was listening to every word she said. She continued, "I hated God for this. Men raping me and making me be with them; being forced to serve my father as if he were an animal in a cage; watching my mother abused and beaten. And I never saw God stop any of this."

The man began to cry, as his daughter went on. "But I have listened to these men. They live out everything you ever taught me and I again believe that Jesus is my king. It is through His strength and my faith in him that I am able to go on in this. I do not like this life I have, but remembering the things that you, my father, taught me, I am able to go on with joy in my heart and strength in my bones. And mother is, too.

She, too, has recommitted herself to Jesus and we pray and worship together."

The guard saw that she was lingering here and talking. He came running up yelling for her to be quiet and get back to work. She started to turn away when she suddenly looked back; "Daddy, remember Jesus, he loves you."

The guard yelled again at her and slapped her, knocking her down. She quietly gathered up her bucket and stood up hurrying off to where they kept her.

Our entire cell complex was quiet. Tom took my arm in his hand and whispered, "Pray!" I began to pray quietly as Tom did also.

It was at that point that the man yelled, "O Jesus, forgive me!" I looked up startled at the intensity of his booming voice. His hands were palm upward to heaven. He was on his knees, staring upwards. Streams of tears flowed down his face. I have never seen anyone cry out to Jesus with the intensity that this man did. He flung his head and arms forward to the floor. Kneeling there prostrate before the Lord, he repented and took the first steps to return to the way of Jesus, the way of life.

As that man prayed, Tom and I sat quietly praying and rejoicing that Jesus had touched that man. As we were quietly praying, the man in Tom's cell whispered, "I want to know Jesus, too. I want the peace and joy that you men have."

Tom began to talk with the man. All of the other men listened quietly as Tom spoke. Tom began at the beginning and how God created us and never wanted us to have a life filled with hardship and difficulty. He shared how the Dark Prince; Satan, tempted man and man choose to rebel against God and His holy standard. He talked about the first murder and how the world became increasingly dark and filled with all kinds of evil. He went on to explain how God chose a people for Himself and led them out of captivity. How He gave them laws and standards to live by. Tom explained to the captive audience how these laws could not be kept no matter how hard we tried. They were just too lofty for us who were born in sin. He showed that we could not be restored to who God had originally created us to be on our own. That is when He began to reveal Jesus. He talked of the Bible and history and the evidence that showed that Jesus was the only one that could be the Savior. That is when he explained that the only thing one must do to be saved is to confess their sinfulness to God and ask His forgiveness, accepting the free salvation that Jesus gave us by being the one punished for our sin so that we could live.

Several of the men accepted Christ as their Savior right then and there. Sitting in the damp, humid, jungle cage; filled with the stench of our sweat and overflowing toilet buckets, we found the greatest reason in the world to celebrate-the birth of a new brother or sister into the kingdom of God! With that, we all began to sing the songs that Tom and I had been singing. You would have thought we were having a party, and the guards must have thought we were, because they came running up to the jail complex. They were yelling for us to be quiet and to stop our singing. They were filled with rage as they came rushing up to us. They had sticks and beat on the cage bars demanding that we be quiet. They smelled like beer and slurred their speech as they yelled. The man on the end, whose daughter had scolded him, rose up and stared preaching the hope of Jesus. His voice was filled with life and he bellowed when he spoke. This inflamed the guards. They unlocked his door and flung his roommate against the barred wall and snatched up the man. They drug him off. The whole time he never ceased in his preachings. We continued to praise God if only a little more reserved than before. The whole time Robert sat stoic faced and refused to say anything. At least he wasn't cursing God like he normally did.

Time passed and we all prayed for the man who was drug away. His name, it turned out was Steve. More specifically, Stephen Ryswick, a writer from England. He had been traveling on his sailing yacht with his family, his wife and two daughters, when they had been taken. I thought of how ironic it was that his name was Stephen, the same name as the first martyr in the new church. I wondered what they were doing to him. It was late at night when they returned him. He was drug between two men. They each had an arm and his feet were dragging behind him. His head was drooped down in front of him as if he were unconscious. Obviously he was still alive and conscious, we could hear his continued groanings. He was saying something, but we really couldn't tell what. The guards tossed him into the cell and locked the door. His roommate rushed over to check on him as soon as the guards left. He almost shouted when he said "Praise God! He is saying Praise God!"

We all started praising God again. Steve was alive and still praising God.

As our excitement wound down, we lay in our cots. The way it was set up, two men had to share one large cot. Robert and I barely fit on our cot because we were both big men. I decided that I would lie down on the floor tonight and let Robert have the cot to himself. He asked if I was sure I wanted to do that. I told him that it was okay.

I was just at that point of drifting off when I heard a voice whispering. I slowly shook the sleep from my head when I heard Robert whispering repeatedly, "Johnny! Johnny, are you awake?"

"Yes, I am now," I replied groggily.

He hesitated, "I can't go on like this man. I, I..." He paused for a long moment. "I need what you have, I need this Jesus."

I sat up. I was fuzzy with sleep but I was also excited. "Are you sure?" I asked him. "Yes," he responded with more confidence than he had asked the first time. I was so excited. I quickly shook off the sleep and moved closer to Robert. I led him in a prayer of repentance. My heart was beating in my throat as I listened to his heart-felt prayer. When he finished he looked up at me with the brightest face I think I had ever seen. I suddenly jumped up and shouted "Hallelujah!"

The guards immediately started yelling for me to be quiet. I dropped back down beside Robert and began to laugh quietly. I hugged him, my new brother. Tears of joy streamed down his face.

We didn't get much sleep that night. Morning came far too quickly. The guards were especially agitated. They came up to our cages quickly and opened the doors before our morning feeding had come. They began yelling at us to come out and go to work. We were being punished for our worship service last night. It was okay, it was worth it. Every man in our group of cells had surrendered his life to Jesus! What more could we ask for?

Steve was also expected to work. We all took turns helping him to walk and steadying him as he worked. All of us sang praise songs as we worked. By lunch time the humidity grew so bad that everyone of us was on the verge of collapse. That's when one of the men came hurriedly up and spoke to our overseer. Next thing we knew is we were all being rushed back to our cells. We didn't have to wait long to find out what was going on. The sky blackened quickly as a terrible storm was moving in from the west. We saw the lightning flash across the sky. Before the storm reached the shore, we could see the frothing sea. This was going to be a bad, bad storm.

No sooner had the guards returned us to our cages when the rain hit. It was an immediate downpour. The steel roof over our head echoed with a deafening roar as the massive raindrops came crashing down. The flashes of lightening were blinding and the explosion of thunder shook everything. We all came to the corners of where our cages met with the surrounding cages, and huddled together to pray and have the security of human contact. This broke us up into two groups.

In no time at all the wind hit hard. The rain was driven hard in sheets. The tops of palm trees were ripped off and flung against our cages. Soon entire trees came crashing down. I now understood why all the buildings, including our cages were built up off of the ground. The sea jumped over its boundaries and all of the ground on our tiny island paradise was covered with sea water.

As our tiny group huddled together, we could hear only the roar of the wind, the violence of the sea, and the crashing of thunder. Talking to one another was out of the question. We could barely hear one another when we would shout as loud as we could. The worst of the storm raged on for probably about two hours. It was like a sigh of relief when the worst blew over and the skies settled into a constant downpour.

All of us were alive and well. Well, considering we were imprisoned on a tiny jungle island in the South Pacific somewhere; half starved, barely clothed, beaten and abused, and now half drowned; we were in pretty good shape. As we looked around outside of our cells and saw all the devastation that surrounded us, our faces had to show the amazement we felt. Everywhere we looked we saw trees strewn into heaps. Buildings that used to be there were now gone.   Some had their roofs ripped off, others were collapsed, and some had just vanished. It was as if the hand of God had destroyed everything except our tiny chain of prison cages. Tom and I stood and began to sing a praise song to Jesus for his protection. All the other men followed our lead and before you knew it, we were having a worship service in the middle of all this devastation. We all stood there, rain soaked, with our hands lifted high, praising the God of creation. We were His and we all knew it. They may be able to imprison us; able to beat and abuse our bodies; but we were not forgotten by God! He demonstrated his love for us in the wrath of this storm. It was the prisoners who loved Him that were protected, yet the entire world around us had suffered His punishing wrath.

I wonder if this was what Moses felt like as he stood in the middle of the aftermath of the plagues of God against Pharaoh. Like when all the cattle and livestock were struck dead in the land. All except the cattle and livestock that belonged to the chosen people of God. We were God's chosen people here and we were excited. We worshiped until we had no more energy, and then slowly, one by one, we lay down and went to sleep. God was good.

There was no wake-up call in the morning. No warm rice and warm water brought to us. In fact, we saw no one. The rain had stopped at some point during the night. The sky today was still dark and overcast, but there was no rain. We waited and waited, watching all around us for any sign of life. We saw none. By midafternoon we began to suspect that we were the only ones here. Perhaps God had destroyed everyone else? But what of the women who were believers? There were two at least that we knew of. We sat there talking amongst ourselves about what may have happened. Maybe they all evacuated. Maybe they were all hiding at some safe place in the jungle. Maybe there was a city on the other side of this island. Maybe, maybe, maybe. What if, could be, do you think? All these things were tossed back and forth.

I do not know how long we sat around discussing these possibilities when we heard Robert shout Halleluiah! We all turned at once to the sound of his voice only to see him slipping out from between the bars of our cell. In a flash his feet hit the ground and he stood on the outside looking in. He was grinning from ear to ear. I couldn't think. He was outside the cage looking through the bars at me. "How could this be?" I thought. I heard in the background some of the men asking what he thought he was doing and why had he done this. Robert broke the shock we were all in when he said to me, "Are you coming or are you staying?"

I burst out laughing! I said, "I'm coming brother!" With that, I slid out the opening he had made. The others immediately turned and rushed to the bamboo bars that were lashed together and began working on them to get free. Robert and I went and helped everyone.

It was strange. We had become so used to being a captive that when there were no longer any guards around or people, we just sat in our cages. We had become like animals trained to stay in the cage. When the owner left the door unlocked we didn't move. Praise God for Robert! There is no telling how long we would have sat there waiting for our jailers to come and feed us or tell us what to do.

Once out, we all got together. We had to decide what to do next. Did we search for survivors in this mess? Some of the men had family still here somewhere. Did any boats survive the storm? Could there be a friendly place to go for help on this island? We had to come up with a plan. Tom raised his voice to get everyone's attention. "We are brothers, and it was our God who spared us. We must work together and support one another in this. The decisions we make must be as one body. This is who we are."

The plan that was made was pretty straight forward and simple. Two teams made of two men each would escape to the docks and find some means of escaping this island and going for help. The rest of us would search for our families. If possible we would escape the island also. If not, we would hide in the jungle. If we were recaptured, at least we would have the other two teams that went for help.

www.mickeywilcox.org

Tom and I were looked to as the leaders of our small band of believers. So Tom would leave with one of the teams that were to escape the island. I would stay with the search party. We all huddled together for one last word of prayer before we broke to go about our assigned tasks.

CHAPTER 4

THE PLAGUE!

Sometimes being a man means standing up for what is right, even if it seems wrong to everyone else around you. This rule sounds easy enough, but what if what is right goes against all common sense? Right and wrong is defined by the kingdom we live in. Right, in the kingdom of God is often different than the kingdom of man and is always different from the kingdom of the Dark Prince. What can make perfect logical sense in the kingdom of man can be foolishness in the kingdom of God. I think

www.mickeywilcox.org

this is part of what it means when God says, "My ways are higher than your ways."

This is where I was as we huddled together to pray. We were about to launch out on a plan that seemed logical and correct. However, there was a problem. At least for me there was.

I had made a commitment to God to not leave until these people released me or they had given their life to him. Now I was breaking that commitment. Technically, I wasn't. I was to remain on the island. Well, unless of course we found a way to get everyone off. Then I would be leaving the island. The problem was our captors had not let us go nor had they given their life to Christ. I could make the argument that God had freed us through the storm. But that didn't nullify my commitment to God to remain until these men freed me or gave their life to Him.

It would be so much easier to shut up and go along with our plan. It was a good plan and made sense. But I was a kingdom man. That meant I had honor and integrity. I would do what is right by my king regardless of who was watching or what the circumstances were. If I didn't follow through with my commitment to God, what good were my promises to anyone else?

When we finished praying, I asked for the men's attention for a moment. "Brothers," I said, "I cannot leave with you. I will help us carry out our plan, but when you leave, I will stay here. I made a commitment to God to stay with our captors until they released me or until they gave their life to Jesus. That is why I am here. Know that I love you brothers, and pray for me as I do this. Pray that I will be filled with courage and that God will deliver our captors into his kingdom quickly. Pray that the Dark Prince is unable to stand against me in this, and that I will walk in the power of the Holy Spirit."

Immediately, Tom said that he couldn't leave either and he assigned another brother to the boat crew. Robert spoke up saying that Jesus had saved him too and he surely couldn't abandon the work of his king. Each in his turn said that he could not leave and abandon us or this noble crusade. We decided on a new plan. We would search for all the survivors and care for them as best we could. A couple men went to erect a makeshift shelter from the debris. The rest of us were to gather supplies and survivors.

We did not find many injured. In fact we did not find many people at all. The injured we brought to our makeshift building that became our first-aid station. We tended to their wounds as best that we could. I became our head doctor. It was surprising to see how much the first aid training from the Kingdom Disciples program came into play here. I remember as we went through all the emergency field first aid training that I kept thinking; "Are we really going to ever use all this information?" Here I am today moving around like I actually knew what I was doing. I was surprising even myself. We had nothing to start a fire with and everything was soaked. I had no way of boiling water or cleaning the rags we were using for bandages. We all just did the best we could do under the circumstances. I prayed for each man or woman patient. Every one of them thanked me and said that they already felt better. I prayed over the water that we were cleaning their wounds with and over the rags we used for bandages. We prayed over everything. We would occasionally hear a shout of joy as a father was reunited with a daughter or a wife. It was amazing how wonderful God was in this kind of situation. It wasn't long before people soon came out of the jungle; men, woman, and children. They came to our makeshift camp. We had nearly no supplies, but they trudged through the mud to come to our outpost. Those that could, helped out, those who couldn't, we took care of. The rain had started again so we used old roofing steel to collect the water. We prayed with everyone here. We did the best we could to comfort the sick and injured. Tomorrow we would need a new plan. We were becoming overwhelmed with the number of people to care for. We had fashioned bamboo platforms for the people to lay on that were up off the ground. Many of us went back to our jungle cages to sleep in. They were relatively dry and we were already used to sleeping there. Off and on all night the rain came down. Not in the torrents it had come earlier. More like gentle songs as they played their tune on the steel roofing.

The rain became like a lullaby as we lay there. It was a sing-song tune that quickly put our exhausted bodies to sleep. Pleasant dreams filled my night. I dreamt of home and being a boy again. I was riding my bicycle on a dirt road. It was a summer day and the wind was blowing through my hair. The sun was shining brightly as I peddled as hard as I could down a long slow grade. My friend Billy Hanks was there riding beside me. We were daredevils! We would race down the roads as fast as we could and jump across the creeks and anything else we could find. We had set up some old plywood and a concrete cinder block we had found and built a ramp. We were going to jump the ditch and land in the old bean field. Our imaginary crowd would go wild at our display of courage! We jumped side by side and flew through the air! Side by side Billy and I flew. It was exhilarating. We landed hard on two wheels as our bicycles made the jump. Stepping down and backward we locked up the rear tires on our mighty steeds of light-weight metal and rubber. Our rear tires slid in unison as we braked hard. Together we slid to a stand-still. My face was beaming. I looked at Billy as we prepared to throw our hands up and make the sound of applause of our imaginary crowd. Billy turned and looked at me, but his face looked different. His eyes were hard and narrow. In a voice I didn't recognize, the voice of a hard man, he said, "Get up!" Suddenly my body began to shake as if the whole world were caught up in an earthquake. I grabbed my handlebars and yelled "Billy!" With a start I opened my eyes. Wide eyed I looked around. Robert was shaking my leg. Again he said firmly, "Get up!" I sat up and looked at the barrel of an AK-47 and up into the burning eyes of one of our captors.

Morning brought a beautiful day. A cool breeze was blowing in gently off of the Pacific Ocean. The sun was bright with just a few white puffy clouds here and there. The jungle had come back to life. You could hear the birds singing and the palm leaves softly whispering in the breeze. The morning also brought out our captors. They had fled in a big power boat shortly after they got us back into our cages. They had fled to some place of safety while leaving all of us here to fend for ourselves. They seemed somewhat confused and unsure of what to do. We seem to have confused them. They found us alive and able to escape, yet we were still here. There were about a half dozen armed guards surrounding us. We were all on our knees in a line. Hands tied behind our backs. We were not allowed to look up so we couldn't see very much of what was going on. They were pretty harsh in getting us all corralled into this line. The women were once again separated. The fathers and husbands were beaten pretty badly for their indiscretion. As they were being punished, we could hear the leader of these bandits telling them over and over that these women no longer belonged to them. They had stolen another man's woman. They would kick them and tell them that they were slaves and could not be husbands and fathers. Real men would never have given up their ship and family, we were just cowards and spineless dogs. We deserved to be here.

Suddenly Steve shouted back at the guard beating him. "You are wrong! She is my wife, bone of my bones and flesh of my flesh. That is my daughter. A treasure that God has given to me and you will know the vengeance of God for what you have done!" He spat on the ground. His outburst resulted in a butt stroke to the side of the head with an Ak-47. He immediately fell unconscious to the ground. I shouted "Praise God! Jesus is King!" I couldn't control my outburst. The courage of Steve to defend the truth in the face of such terror, made me have to do something. My something was rewarded with my own butt stroke from an AK-47. The hard wood rifle butts were like a blow from nothing I have ever felt before. When it hit, my brain exploded in a blinding flash of light. I couldn't see anything for a moment. I regained my senses as I lay face first in the mud gagging on the water and filth I lay in. The sound of the bandit leader was all I could hear. "No more! No more!" he said.

"We will need them to do work; we have to get back up and running quickly."

After our cells were repaired we were taken back to them and locked up. The guards would only come and get a few of us at a time. They would take us out on work details to clean up debris and gather the scattered supplies. Our work went well into the night. By the time they let us rest, it had to be well after midnight.

In the morning we were brought warm rice and warm water. The rice was soggy and was probably bad rice. It had dirt and sand mixed into it. I would say that it was rice they had found in the dirt. At least it was something. We hadn't eaten in a very long time and we were starving. After we were given some time to eat, we were again taken out for forced labor. Today our men were forced to exhume the dead bodies buried in the rubble. There were far more than anyone would have guessed. It was easy to tell where they were because in this tropical heat you could smell them. We would have to carry the bodies into the jungle and dig holes to bury them. It was the worst kind of work. We prayed continually in those days. The guards would randomly stop us and beat us. It was as if they blamed us for the storm. These were truly days of sorrow for us.

On about the third day, I was taken to see the bandit leader. I was thrown down in front of him. He sat in a chair at a table drinking a warm beer. He looked sickly as did all the guards. Normally we were not allowed to look at them but for some reason they didn't mind right now.

There were others in the little roofed pavilion style building. Some of them I recognized as people who were in our little impromptu field hospital. They looked like they were doing very well. Their faces were healthy and it appeared as though all their wounds had healed well. The bandit leader scowled at me, "Did you fix these people?"

"Well," I began, "God did, but yes I did what I could medically for them."

He kicked me. "I don't want to hear about your God!" he shouted. "What medicine did you give them?"

"None." I replied. "I washed their wounds and wrapped them with whatever we could find then I prayed for God to heal them."

"I don't want to hear about your stupid God!" He said even more angrily. "Are you a doctor?"

"No." I said

"What are you?" he asked.

"I am just a man sent by God." I answered as boldly as I could knowing that I was probably going to get hit for my answer.

He kicked me again, only this time hard enough to knock me backwards. I fell backwards into the dirt. "Why didn't you leave when you could have?" he asked.

Lying on my back and side with my head lifted up to be able to see him; I answered, "Because I was sent by God to tell you about his love for you."

That was it. He heard enough. He was hoppin' mad! He jumped up and threw his half empty beer bottle at me. I tried to dodge it but having your hands tied behind your back while lying on the ground made it really difficult. The bottle slammed into my chest. It knocked the wind out of me for a moment. The beer poured out all over me as the guards stooped to grab my arms and drag me back to my cell. Suddenly, the leader spun around and shouted "Wait!" "Some of my men are getting sick. You will treat them or I will torture you and your friends." He looked at his guards. "Take him to our sick comrades. Get him what he needs. If he runs, start shooting his friends. Start with the one he came with." With that he turned and walked away.

I was taken to a makeshift infirmary. There were three men in there that appeared to be very sick. There were about ten people sitting outside the infirmary on a little porch that I could tell were not doing much better than the men inside. They were all ashen faced and coughing. This was far more than I could handle. These people were suffering from some kind of tropical sickness. It was probably brought on by the hurricane style storm and the dead animals and people ripening in the sun and the heat. We would be lucky if everyone didn't get whatever it is and die. "O Lord," I said, "I'm gonna need a miracle."

I began by checking the men inside. They were burning up with fever. Their eyes were bloodshot and their breathing was raspy and short. They had a stench about them like a fever smell. I got some rags dipped in water and placed it on their heads. I gave a woman they assigned to work with me, a bowl of water and told her what to do. She looked pretty sick herself, but she could stand. On the porch I examined each one of the others. Everyone had a fever, raspy breathing, and complained of flu-like symptoms. Their breath all had the same putrid smell to it. We would need lots of clean water, antibiotics, and more space. We truly needed a real doctor. I wasn't even a medic. I was just a man that knew some basic first aid. Why couldn't they understand, I didn't heal those people, God did. "O God", I cried out, "Help me, help these people." I told the guard that I needed antibiotics, like penicillin. I also needed clean water, a lot of it. I would need clean rags and needed much more space. I had to yell to the guard because he would not come near me.

About one hour later I was brought clean white sheets that looked like they were stolen from a hotel. They brought buckets of water. And they brought about a dozen more victims. I asked about the antibiotics. They told me they had not been able to find any. I tried to explain that without the medicine these people were probably going to die. All I could do was comfort them.

Their leader came up to me. He looked really bad, and very angry. "If you do not heal my men," he said, "I will kill your people; starting with your friend."

"That's not going to help anyone." I said.

One of his men brought Tom over and forced him to his knees. He put his AK-47 to the back of Tom's head and stood there.

"It's okay son," said Tom calmly. "I am ready. A crown of life waits for me." With that he closed his eyes and began to softly sing.

I looked at the bandit leader. He looked at Tom and then at me. "Fix my men." He said as he stormed off.

The guard released Tom who then got up. Tom came over and said "let me help you." The guard seemed content to let Tom and I work together un-harassed. We quickly went to work trying to comfort those who were sick. When we did all we could do, we began to pray over each one. We would kneel beside them and cry out to God on their behalf. Those who were conscious would weep with streams of tears while we prayed.

Tom and I were forced to sleep there in the infirmary. We found a spot on the floor and curled up and slept fitfully. Sleep was not my friend tonight. I had troubled dreams all night long. They were funny dreams. Not laughing funny, but strange. It was like there was this war going on in my dreams all night long. Later Tom told me that I would wake up moaning and sometimes crying out to Jesus. I had never before experienced anything like it.

Morning brought us ten more patients. Many of those yesterday who were just feverish, were now unconscious. Ironically, none of the men and women who were believers got sick. Other than Tom and I being hungry all the time, we felt fine. The hunger was normal; we had grown used to it. We had received one small portion of rice each yesterday afternoon, and no rice at all this morning.

About mid-afternoon I was summoned by a guard to follow him. He took me into a separate shelter. There, lying on a bed, was the leader of the bandits. He looked very bad. His breathing was shallow and labored. The guard said, "Stay with him. When he dies, all of you prisoners die." Then the guard turned and left the room. It was just me and this man who had brought all this trouble on us.

God calls us to show mercy to our enemy. In this way we heap coals of punishment upon their heads.

That's easy to say, but I watched as this man calmly shot Patty because Tom wouldn't lie and tell the insurance company that the boat had been lost in a storm. He was an animal and if anyone on this island deserved a slow terrible death, surely it was him. I stood there unmoving for the longest time. I wouldn't even wipe his brow with a damp cloth to try and cool his fever. All I wanted to do was clamp my hand over his mouth and watch as he struggled for breath and died.

CHAPTER 5

FREEDOM

My mind wrestled for what seemed like an eternity. It was as if there were two of me; a good side and a bad side. The good side kept reminding me of who I was and what I should be doing. The bad side kept telling me why I was justified in letting him die. This was the hardest mental battle I had ever faced. In the midst of this swirling mental battle came what I can only describe as the voice of God. In a gentle voice that I heard at least in my spirit, but I would not have been surprised if it was audible; "Who are you son?" That was it; four little words. My entire life revolved around those four little words. The answer to that question would define who I was. No amount of good or bad could do what the answer to those words could do. I thought I had answered that question a long time ago when I accepted Jesus into my life. However, here and now I was faced with the real choice. I did not understand why God had allowed me to be in this situation or why God allowed Patty to die. I did not understand so much about all of this, but I did understand one thing. I was a kingdom man. I belonged to Jesus and it was for his purpose that I lived and died. This man lying here in front of me was a terrible man. He inflicted hurt and pain for fun. He was a thief and a liar, a murderer and rapist. He deserved to suffer and die. But then, so did I. Jesus took my punishment upon Himself for me and He took this man's punishment if he was willing to give it to Jesus. Jesus loved him and it was my job to bring him the love of Christ no matter what he deserved. My mind was made up. I am a kingdom man, a man of character and integrity. I work for the King of kings and will serve Him. With that I took a rag and began to wipe the man's forehead.

As I wiped his head, he began to speak. He was weak. I smiled and told him to be quiet. "You will be fine," I said gently, filled with a compassion I didn't know I had. "Today you will not die. That God you do not believe in is going to heal you and give you back your life. I am here to bring you His love."

His eyes filled with tears as I wiped him down to help comfort him. I prayed and sang as I wiped. "O Jesus," I cried, "heal this man and give him back his life. Let him see your mercy. If someone must die, let it be me. Give me his sickness and suffering. You know that I am yours, that I belong to you. For me there is nothing but life forever with you. For him, there is just eternal darkness and damnation. Do not allow him to pass through the door of death to spend forever there; breathe life back into him."

When I could no longer stand, I brought a chair over from the corner and sat it next to his bed. I washed him frequently and kept him as comfortable as possible. Either God would heal him, or, I and my brothers would be dead by morning. It was out of my hands.

I drifted off to sleep there in the chair. I don't remember when or at what time. I was startled when a strong pair of hands grabbed my shoulders and shook me awake. "Wake up!" demanded the gruff voice. I looked up dropping the bowl and rag in my hand. There in front of me sitting upright in his bed was the bandit leader. "Stay here," he commanded. He really didn't have to tell me that because I wasn't sure I could move. It was like witnessing a resurrection. He looked as healthy as he ever did. He rose up out of his bed and walked out the door. I wasn't sure what to do. I dropped to my knees and thanked God for His miraculous power! Who besides God can sweep death away?

Outside I heard many cheers and sounds of celebration. I just continued to wait in this building until his return. I sang and praised Jesus with all my heart. I had been in this one room building for probably an hour when the door opened up. It was one of the guards. He said to follow him. I noticed that instead of carrying his machine gun it was slung over his shoulder. As we walked, I could hear the sound of one of the big inboard power boats they used for their pirate raids driving off into the distance. The atmosphere felt different and I could feel my anxiety level raising. As we walked, I began to see other people all walking in the same direction. The atmosphere was happy and crackled with an excitement. You would have thought we were on our way to a party; except, of course, I was being escorted by an armed guard. We finally came to a large court yard where they would sometimes bring us to punish us or to punish one person to set an example. I saw all my brothers lined up there. The bandit leader waved me forward to come up to him. He stood up and with his hand turned me around. He placed his hand on my shoulder as if we were friends and faced the crowd. I wasn't sure what was going to happen but I wasn't real comfortable right at that moment. I said a silent prayer to Jesus for Him to strengthen me.

The bandit leader began to speak. "I am Bong Arnauta, prince of this island and of these people. We have been pirates for generations. We live by taking the ships that trespass in our part of the sea. The men work as slaves and the woman are sold as such. Today is a new day. Last night I was about to die. This man here before you was brought to me to heal me. I left orders that if I should die all of the men you see lined up would also be killed. But this man did not heal me. Instead, he gave me comfort. He wiped my forehead with water to cool me and gave me water to sip so I would not be thirsty. He cried out to his God who I did not believe in to heal me. I heard him say that if someone had to die that it would be better if his God would kill him and spare me. I have never heard a man do that for his master and owner. This man was my slave who I treated very badly and still he was willing to die for me."

"I thought he was foolish when I heard him pray. I tried to laugh at him but I could not speak. Last night, his God came to me and touched me and spared my life. I saw Him as a man, only He appeared bright as the sun and it was as if he were on fire. His hand touched my forehead and he said, "Be healed." After that I was healed and I sat up on my bed. I saw this man still sitting in a chair beside me. He still held the bowl of water that he would dip his rag in to cool my head.   His other hand still held the rag. His lips still moved saying his prayer for me. Today, I know there really is a God and it is this man's God. From today on, I will serve this God and any people here on my island must serve this God also. Anyone who does not want to serve this God must leave my island. We will no longer be pirates and slave traders. We will serve this man's God as he does. Although they were captives, this man and his friend from the same ship have always been filled with joy and love for their God. We have been unable to take that from them; they always sing and pray. Their love for their God spread to the other slaves and they, too, would become joyful even though they were prisoners. As slaves they would no longer rebel against us or try to escape. When this last great storm hit, they alone were spared. Yet even then, they did not try to escape. They stayed and cared for many of you. When the sickness came, they cared for the sick, even the very men that abused them. Men do not do these things. I see now that they did this because of their God who is now my God and the God of my people."

With that he sat down as all the people cheered. He looked at me and asked, "Will you stay and teach us about your God that we may know Him like you do?" How could I possibly say no? So I said yes. He called over one of his guards and spoke to him briefly.

The guard ran off hurriedly towards the dock. Bong stepped down and walked towards my brothers who were once prisoners. He took my arm so that I would walk with him. He nodded at one of his guards as we stopped in front of the men. The guard rushed behind each man and untied them while one of the native women brought clean clothes to the men.

"I give you my apologies. I see now that what I have done to you and your families was wrong. I can never repay you for what I have taken from you. Please forgive me." said Bong. He spoke with all the regal authority of a king. If this were a different time, he probably would have been a great king. Here, on this tiny island in the South Pacific, Bong Arnauta was a prince. He continued on. "For some of you, your wives and daughters are here. They are free to return to you. For some of you, your women have been sold. My men are now, searching for them to return them to you. For some of you, I still have your vessel, for others I do not. For those whose vessels I have, they will be returned to you. For those whose vessel I do not have, I will give you one of my nicest vessels. I can never repay all that has been taken, but I will repay all that I can."

It was surreal, as if we were not completely here. Almost dream-like. We were all moved from our jungle cages of bamboo and brought into other people's homes as honored guests. Husbands and wives were reunited. Fathers and daughters were reunited again with long embraces and cries of joy. For some of the families, it took several days for the families to be reunited. However, Bong was true to his word. Every wife and daughter that had been sold was bought back and returned. Every boat that had been taken had been returned.

Bong never let me leave his side. He questioned me from early morning until late at night everyday about Jesus and the Bible. He devoured everything I had to teach. Every evening at dinnertime the whole village from the island would gather together and we would worship. Tom and I and Robert would take turns teaching the word of God. This would usually last for hours until it was late and we could no longer stay awake. The next day would find Tom and Robert with groups of men and women gathered around them seeking to understand more about Jesus. It quickly got to the point that we saw no more weapons or armed guards. This entire tiny island had been sold out to Jesus!

I had read stories of mass conversions, but this was the first time I had ever experienced it. It was crazy. After a week, Robert, Tom and I talked about baptizing all these new believers. We explained baptism to Bong and asked if there were a place on the island that had a fresh water hole deep enough to baptize everyone. Bong showed us a great big fresh water hole, complete with waterfall. It was beautiful, probably the most beautiful baptismal I had ever seen. It was big enough that all three of us could baptize people at the same time.

A day was chosen for this big baptismal ceremony. Robert, Tom, and I taught in depth about baptism and the significance of it. We taught the people how it was not the act of baptism that saved you. It was representative of the transition from the old life into the new life. We explained how it was the first act of obedience and a public demonstration of a person's commitment to follow the ways of Christ.

On the day of baptism, we all woke up early. As we walked through the jungle to our baptism hole, the people began to sing. As the procession of people flowed through the jungle like a trail of army ants, the sounds of their singing drowned out all the normal jungle sounds. I thought to myself, "This is the sound of God's army marching forward." I knew that there would come many difficulties and hardships for these people in the future, but for today, it was a mountain-top experience.

The crowd surrounded the large pond that was now our baptismal. Robert, Tom, and I waded out into the pond up to our waist. Robert, being in the middle, he climbed up a rock that was centrally located beneath the waterfall. He spread out his arms and began to speak. "Brothers and sisters," he began with a great resonating voice amplified because of the backdrop of rock. "today you gather to be baptized into the kingdom of God. For any of you who have not turned away from your sins, from your ways that are contrary to the way of God and asked Jesus to forgive you of your evil ways of the past; this is not for you to partake in. Today is a day for the believer in Jesus. For you, the believer, today marks a great day on your journey to walk in righteousness. Today you will make a public confession of your trust in Jesus as your King. The dunking of your body into the water represents your old life being laid into the grave. When you burst forth out of the water, it represents a new and redeemed life walking in truth before Jesus Christ your King. From this point forward, you will walk in His ways and honor Him in everything you do. You will follow all of His teachings we have given to you and live according to those teachings. May peace follow each of you all the days of your life."

With that, he stepped back down into the water. I had never heard such a speech given before a baptism. It was wonderful and something I will never soon forget. As Robert resumed his place, the crowd began to come forward. Individuals and families came forward, each taking their turn to be baptized. Bong came to me. He said, "Brother, I would be honored if you would baptize me into the kingdom of God." I smiled and embraced him and said, "I would be the one who is honored, brother."

After hours of baptizing people, we went back to our village. There the women prepared a great feast. We all sang and celebrated the rest of the day. It was hard to imagine that not very long ago; this island knew no laughter from joy. It was hard to remember that the trials of the past months were real. As we celebrated with these people who were bubbling over with joy and love; we could not see the violence and hate that once were in them. God had truly done an amazing thing here. As I sat there reflecting on this thing that God had done, I was overcome with an awe of who God is. I excused myself and went over to where my old cell stood, door hanging open, and knelt down inside of it. I began to worship Jesus on my face. Streams of tears flowed from my eyes. It was if I were in the very presence of God. I could not have gotten up if I had wanted to. I couldn't look up. It was as if God was right there and if I looked up, I would die because of His brilliance. So I lay on the floor of my old cell and worshiped my King.

I have no idea how much time had passed, but when I got up, it was quiet out with only the noises of the night. I walked back to Bong's house where I saw him sitting on one chair with an empty chair beside him. I walked up on his porch and sat down in the empty chair. He handed me a warm Coke which I gladly accepted. I thanked Jesus for it and popped off the top. We sat there in silence for a short time while we sipped on our warm Coke bottles. Bong finally broke the silence. "Brother," he began, "you must make plans to leave soon. You must go back to your life and the work you do for our King. Tomorrow, I shall present Brother Tom with a sailing ship. It is not the one that I took from him, but it is a very nice one. His ship I could not find no matter how much I looked for it. I think he will like it. We have completely refinished it and even now as we speak, some of my men are sailing it here to my island. I will give it to him in the morning after breakfast. Then, the two of you will be able to leave. Some of the others are already talking of leaving. I think it is time. My people will have a long way to travel on our new path. Tomorrow morning our first shipment of Bibles comes. It will be a wonderful gift for all of my people. Many of them cannot read. Only myself and one or two others can read, but I thought that my people would like to have the Holy Book anyway. I will teach the people the best I can. I do give you my word, brother, we will not go back to our old ways. We will serve Jesus with all of our hearts and minds and bodies."

I looked at Bong for a long moment and finally said, "I believe you, Bong. You are a good man and will be a great leader to your people." With that, I turned my head to look back at the direction I had come from. I sipped my Coke quietly. I was trying to wrap my head around what had just happened back at the old bamboo cell. I was rested and full of energy. There was nothing I could reason out. Somehow I felt completely recharged.

CHAPTER 6

AWKWARD MOMENTS

My thoughts were interrupted by the realization that the sun was rising. "How could that be?" I thought aloud. I turned my head to see if Bong was still beside me. He was sitting there very peacefully.

"How can what be?" he asked.

"The sun," I said in shock, "it's rising."

"Brother Johnny, you spent the whole night praying over there at the jail. Some of us came and began to pray after many others left to go to bed. We prayed for many hours with you, then we left. You never moved. You prayed as if you were talking directly to Jesus, as if you were right there. None of us dared go near you for fear that you were with God. When we finished we returned. I slept here in my chair waiting for your return but you never returned. I was just having a warm coke for breakfast when you did return."

I was stunned. I had been praying all night. Wow! I thought, that had never happened before. God is full of surprises.

Bong went on. "Today, we will tear down the jails. They are what we used to be about. When they are torn down, we will build a church in its spot. It will be what we are about now."

The prince of this island band of seafaring bandits really had been transformed. He was made relatively wealthy and powerful in his old ways. The piracy of sea-going ships that passed by ands the trade in human beings had given him a reputation to be feared. Here today, his old allies would never recognize him. He was a man concerned with the welfare of his people and the honoring of the one true God. I knew I had to leave, and I did want to, but a part of me did not want to. That part of me wanted to stay here and witness what would go on among these people. I would pray that God would send someone mature in the faith to walk along side Bong and his people.

As the sun came up, crews of people could be seen and heard tearing down the old bamboo prisons and preparing to build the new place of worship. Bong and I moved to the covered pavilion area where Bong sat and ruled over his people. It was at this very same spot that Tom and I had first encountered this man. Of course in that day, he was brutal and harsh. It was here that he had shot Patty in the head while she kneeled bound and helpless before him. It was his attempt to force Tom to lie and say his boat had been sunk in a storm and then sign over the insurance money to Bong and his pirates.

Tom had refused, and it had cost him the life of the woman he loved. He never showed any sign of anger toward Bong over this matter. In fact, had I not been there, I would not have believed that the Bong of that day and the Bong of today were the same man and you sure couldn't tell it by Tom.

Bong and I took our normal places at the table. His table used to be surrounded only by his pirate captains, now it was surrounded by his reformed captains, myself, Tom, and Robert. Where the conversation used to be about robbery and rape, it was now filled with legitimate trade, concerns about the people of this island, and Jesus.

When everyone was gathered, we began with a prayer of thanksgiving to God for this day and asking for His guidance in it. Then Bong began to share his plans for the future. They were ambitious in that he wanted to begin sending men and woman throughout all the surrounding islands to carry the message of Christ's love. These were all new believers here and I was concerned for this new church. Left to themselves, they would be vulnerable to false teachings. They really needed some mature leadership to guide them and help them to deal with issues that would come up from time to time. For most believers, it was common to flare up with excitement about Jesus and His kingdom, only to find elements of their past would try to sneak back in to their life. A person needed a strong believing friend to walk alongside during these times to gently remind them who they were. Temptations of our weaknesses from the past were some of the Dark Prince's most effective tools to use against us. I thought to myself that I will have to pray about this for guidance on what to suggest to Bong and the others. It was in the middle of this thought that I heard Tom surprise everyone with his words. "Gentleman," he began, "we have given this much thought and prayer, and Robert and I have decided to remain here on this island to assist with the new church that our glorious Jesus has planted here." He had everyone's attention as he continued. "Brothers, it is important that some of us who have walked with Jesus for a long time remain as your elders. There will be many difficult days ahead and we must walk through these days together, as brothers in the kingdom of God and not fall to the temptations that will lie before us to tarnish this beautiful bride of Christ. Johnny must return to the work he has. Robert and I have nothing to gain by leaving and nothing waiting for us beyond this island. We have both talked and Robert has talked with his family; we all agree that we must stay."

I looked at Tom and then Robert, then my eyes slowly moved to Bong. Streams of tears flowed from this Prince's eyes. He seemed broken at what Tom had just said. I wondered if he was tormented by the memory of the murder he had committed against Patty. I quickly turned my eyes to the reformed captains sitting at the table. Many of them were also either flowing with tears or on the verge of tears. When women cry, it can move a man's heart, but when real men, warrior men, cry, it can break another man.

There was a long moment of silence as we all looked down at the table giving each other respect as they all composed themselves. Bong was the first to recover himself and break the silence. "Men, it is settled. These two men and their families shall remain here among us as our elders to continue to teach us the way of Christ." Bong then began to order some of his men to give Tom and Robert choice pieces of land and to assign people to help them build a house. I wasn't sure what to think. Up until this moment, I had assumed that I would be traveling home with Tom. Especially since just a short time ago, Bong informed me that the *Pearl of Love* was on her way back here. Now I did not know how I would return.

The day passed quickly as we had work to focus on. When not teaching and answering questions about the Word of God, I was helping to build the new worship center.

In the morning everyone came together at the request of Bong. We all gathered together in the courtyard near the docks where I had first met Bong. There parked in the harbor, tied up to the pier, was the *Pearl of Love;* she looked more beautiful than the first time I had ever seen her. I was sure Tom would leap for joy.

When Bong presented her to Tom, he expressed a great deal of joy at seeing her, but I knew that he wasn't as overjoyed as he portrayed. I imagine that it brought back a lot of painful memories of his lost love. Tom thanked Bong for his generosity and thoughtfulness at returning the *Pearl of Love.* In his eyes you could see sadness. I silently prayed for Tom. The loss of Patty would be a deep wound to heal. Would he ever fully heal from this hurt while remaining on the island with Bong, I wondered to myself. "Only if he completely steps into the place of forgiveness," came the unexpected answer deep from within my spirit. I would have to remember to continue to keep Tom in my prayers. Sometimes as strong believers we can know what we should do, but doing it can be hard. I have never experienced the loss that Tom experienced, but I did know that forgiveness can be hard to give and sometimes take time to be fully given. True forgiveness moves the terrible hurts of life into a place where they no longer hurt us and keep us captive and they no longer become an obstacle or justification to keep the other person from the love of Jesus. Tom had set his feet in the right direction for true forgiveness, now it would just take time and commitment.

After Bong had presented Tom with his ship once again, we had a massive feast with everyone from the island in attendance. This was a special going away feast. For those of us leaving, we had come as unwilling captives, but we were leaving as friends and family. There were many embraces and even more tears of love and sorrowful joy that one has in times like these. We would miss these people.

Bong, Tom, and Robert came to sit down with me. We had all become very close over the last few weeks. It is amazing what Jesus does and how He does it. Bong began by saying to me, "Brother, tomorrow morning with the out-going tide, you will be leaving." Tom jumped in, "Robert and his wife will take you to Hawaii on the *Pearl of Love*. She needs her sails stretched and run through the motions. She's been refitted, but I would prefer not to go it alone on the way back. Robert is a skilled seaman and he is still waiting on his sea mistress to come back to him."

Robert took over the conversation, "If you don't mind, brother, it will be you and I and my wife and daughter. We will sail to Hawaii; the journey will take us about two weeks. Afterwards, my wife and I will be returning here. My daughter will be continuing on with you back to the mainland. Please take care of her until she arrives back in Georgia, if you wouldn't mind." I told him that I would look after her. Everything was beginning to feel so final. Not very long ago, I wasn't even sure I would make it off of this island alive. Now, I was supposed to be heading home. God truly does move in some wild ways.

I spent the rest of the day praying over each person there on the island. Early that evening we all gathered under the makeshift roof of the soon-to-be church.

There we had a moving worship service. Bong stood to make the formal announcement that Tom and Robert and Robert's wife would be the leadership team for the island church. He talked at some length about how they would help to guide all the people of the island towards the fulfillment of the vision to reach all the surrounding islands with the message of God's great love and to tell them of the mighty miracles that God had performed here on this island. Afterwards, Tom and Robert, and Robert's wife Nancy, each said a few words of encouragement. Then we all took a seat as the church leaders led us in our first communion as a church. How moving it was as we all broke bread and drank wine in remembrance of Jesus's broken body and shed blood for our sins against God. I am always filled with awe when I take communion and think about the significance of what he did, but none more so than this night. After this communion, we all spent a great deal of time together praying for the church and for each other. We began it by me formally laying my hands on the shoulders of Tom,

Robert, and Nancy, and commissioning them to lead this new church in the true ways of Christ and into the vision that had been given to them. Then the four of us laid our hands on and prayed over Bong and each of his captains. It was late when we finished.

Several hours before dawn, Robert, Nancy, their daughter Shannon, and myself boarded the *Pearl of Love*. As we walked up the dock to the small sailing vessel, the captains lined the gangway. At the end, just where we were to board, stood Tom and Bong. The men each hugged us in turn and somberly boarded the small ship. We shoved off and began to drift out to sea as the tide took us out. We hoisted and set the sails, and before long, the lights of the dock faded from the horizon. Lord willing, I would be in Hawaii in just a couple weeks and from there, I would see my family and home church again for the first time in nearly a year. Would they ever believe all the crazy things I had been through? Sometimes it is hard to believe the impossible occurred even when we know we serve the God where there is no impossible.

I was already anticipating the places God would carry me to next!

END OF

BOOK TWO

Look for Book three to be released soon. Follow the Adventures of Johnny McGinnis as he does what few men are ever willing to do.

www.mickeywilcox.org

Book 1 available on Amazon in paper-back and Kindle format.

www.mickeywilcox.org

Check out other books from Mickey Wilcox.

"THE MOST EXCELLENT WAY"

The true events leading up to and through my personal salvation experience.

"REFLECTIONS ON INTERCESSION"

Journey with me through my experiences in the awesome power of prayer and Intercession.

All books available on Amazon and my web site:

www.mickeywilcox.org

www.mickeywilcox.org

Follow "**12 Minutes With Mickey**" on
Facebook at
www.facebook.com/mickey.wilcox

Check out my website to learn more of the
exciting ministries God has placed in my
life at:
www.mickeywilcox.org

For questions, speaking engagement
schedule, or
to learn more about this amazing Jesus,
email me at:
usmc_mic@hotmail.com